Zone One

A Grenadian short story

By D. E. Ambrose

ISBN: 9781671656895

Ambee Publishing
www.deambrose.net
ambrose.david.e@gmail.com

Cover photo by D. E. Ambrose

Author's photo by Jean Renel Pierre Louis

Map of Grand Anse copied from Google Earth

DEDICATION

This story is dedicated to the law-abiding motorists of Grenada.

.

Zone One

A Short Story

This story is total fiction. The events described never happened. The characters and names do not exist to the best of my knowledge. Incidents are products of my imagination and are used fictitiously. Any resemblance to actual people or events is purely coincidental.

ACKNOWLEDGMENTS

O give thanks unto the Lord, for he is good:
-    Psalms 107: 1

Special thanks to Sergeant Ryan Smith of the Royal
Grenada Police Force for consulting on this story.

A red 2003-model "old school" Toyota Hiace rounded the corner at the southern end of The Carenage in St. George's, Grenada's capital, and approached the Burns Point bus-stop just ahead. Its conductor leaned far out of a window looking for additional fares. A decent mid-morning crowd of seven people waited in the shed.

"Graan' Aanse! Graan' Aanse!" the conductor's squeaky voice reached the gathering. His left index finger pointed in the general direction of Grenada's best beach.

Two Caucasians craned their necks to hear better what the lad shouted. They smiled as an American accent blessed their ears.

"Grend Ense?"

The youth slid open the door before the bus had come to a complete stop. He ignored the black people and addressed the foreigners.

"You guys headin' to the beach?" He smiled at the two young ladies.

Brigitte and Erika, two German visitors, checked the large decal at the top of the vehicle's windshield. A Zone One bus. They looked at each other and nodded.

"Ya, vee vant too go too zee beech," Brigitte said.

The ladies smiled at the passengers as they entered the bus. Most passengers smiled back. As the conductor hopped in after the new commuters, he checked through the back window for his competition and a sound escaped his throat. A bus appeared around the corner and accelerated to pass them.

"Freddy, leh we go," he advised the driver. "Look Ricky and dem comin'. Doh make dem pass us."

The Toyota peeled out, burning tyres on the black road surface and alarming some passengers. The Germans grabbed the handles on the seat in front of them. A blue Nissan eighteen-passenger van attempted to overtake them on the right. The tourists tightened their grip on the handles. Their knuckles whitened. A round-about sat less than ten metres away *and both buses were turning right.* The Nissan slowed to allow the Toyota to pull ahead. Soon both vehicles raced along Port Highway heading south toward Grand Anse. Brigitte glanced at passengers, relaxed her grip and exhaled softly after seeing a sea of calm or expressionless faces. Digital devices occupied some while others stared into space. Both ladies perspired like long distance athletes although the wind blew freely through the interior of the bus. Erika gulped as Freddy flew through an intersection, overtaking a loaded tractor-trailer as they moved through a green light. Both girls grasped their chests as he blasted his electronic horn.

The Toyota and the Nissan leapt-frogged each other as both buses stopped to drop off or pick up passengers along the route.

"Vettel *oder* Hamilton?" Erika nudged her friend while pointing her chin at the driver.

Brigitte laughed. Both ladies chorused, "Lewis Hamilton!"

The ladies conversed excitedly about the experience. They often drove on the *Autobahn* in Germany, but today's bus ride terrified them like never before. And they were yet to get used to driving on the left side of the road. They marvelled at the skill of the driver as he tore around corners or flew by oncoming vehicles on the two-lane road with only centimetres to spare. Four minutes after hopping onto this death-trap, the gleaming white sand of Grand Anse beach came into view.

"*Wir müssen an der Haltestelle bei Morne Rouge aussteigen,*" Erika said to her friend.

Brigitte relayed the request in English to the conductor and soon they stood on solid ground at the Morne Rouge round-about. With shaky legs, they approached a bench to rest. Erika bought glasses of pure cane juice from a vendor. As they guzzled the sweet organic beverage, a uniformed police patrol sped through the round-about and raced after the buses. *Maybe he will give them a ticket for speeding,* Brigitte thought.

****

Corporal Lewis sat high in the saddle of his black and white BMW R1200RT-P motorcycle, grinning like a Cheshire cat, as he left the Morne Rouge round-about in his wake, and headed further south into Grand Anse. His mind took in the traffic while his eyes focused on a red "old-school" bus ahead. He couldn't help reminiscing about the many re-runs of his favourite TV show, *CHiPS*. With his gold mirrored sunglasses, he imagined that he looked like Officer Punch. He chuckled as he gunned the engine to overtake the bus. He anticipated a long and difficult shift today, for it was Christmas Eve. He hoped he didn't have to issue many tickets. He measured the success of his day by the number of tickets he wrote. The fewer citations he gave out and the fewer violations he reported, the better he felt about his patrol. However, his superiors didn't see it that way. They wanted all traffic officers to bring in as much money as possible. The Head of the Traffic Department had once said publicly that his unit should be able to bring in millions of dollars each year for government. The seven-year veteran of the Royal Grenada Police Force smiled as he turned right at the Republic House round-about and onto the Maurice Bishop Highway.

"What the hell!" Corporal Lewis muttered and flipped up the face cover of his black and white modular helmet.

About half a kilometre down the Grand Anse Stretch of the Highway, a Toyota mid-roof bus climbed the 0.3-metre-high and one-metre-wide median to cross from the south-bound to the north-bound lanes. Vehicles coming from further south slowed. Two cars that had accelerated out of the True Blue round-about now had to quickly decelerate. Screeching tyres echoed up and down The Stretch. Ordinarily, vehicles had to travel all the way to the True Blue round-about at the bottom end of The Stretch before driving back up the north-bound side. The white bus stopped halfway up the north-bound side and its driver stared at the motor-officer as the sleek patrol bike sped by. Lewis did a one-eighty at the True Blue round-about and with siren blaring, headed for the passenger vehicle which now pulled away from the bus-stop. The bus eventually stopped a few metres before the Republic Bank round-about.

Corporal Lewis spoke into his radio as he parked his bike behind the bus. Taking his time to dismount, he went through his routine of removing his helmet, resting it on his seat, and extracting his citation book from his saddle bag.

He straightened his black breeches and tightened the blue safety vest that hung over his shirt. A speck of dirt on the "L" in word "POLICE" emblazoned on the lime yellow reflective part on the vest caught his eye and he brushed it off. He turned on the wireless body camera just above his right breast before using the concrete sidewalk to approach the front of the bus. He reminded himself to turn off the device at the end of this traffic stop.

"Driver, what kinda stunt you just pull dey?" Lewis addressed the bearded busman.

Mirrored sunglasses stared back at Corporal Lewis as the driver stroked his beard and sucked his teeth loudly between clenched teeth and pursed lips in a steupse.

"Man, what you talking about?"

Lewis glared at the man through his own shades and shook his head. "Please turn off your engine and hand me your driver's licence and proof of insurance."

The conductor and a few passengers protested loudly, but the driver complied with the order.

"All-you police only dey to harass people," remarked the conductor. "We ha' to make ah money too!"

The driver shoved his credentials toward the police officer. Lewis inspected them, wishing they were invalid in some way. *No such luck*, he thought, after inspecting the documents for a full two minutes.

"Officer, I late for work!" shouted a young lady.

"Driver, please drop all your passengers," Corporal Lewis commanded.

The driver's bottom jaw dropped. "You serious?"

The officer's impassive visage answered the question. The driver gestured to his conductor to let the passengers disembark. A few people shot some curse-words toward Corporal Lewis; he made a mental note of their faces.

"Mr. Joseph," Corporal Lewis said to the bus driver. "I just witness you commit a serious traffic offence a few minutes ago. How you could just drive up on the median to come back up the road?"

"*You* see me drive up on the median?" Joseph's voice increased in volume.

"You coulda *never* see that!" the conductor backed up his driver.

"Well, I did see you. Please step out of the vehicle and onto the sidewalk. You too, Conductor!"

The conductor, a tall, muscular, young man, let loose a string of expletives as he got out of the bus, insulting Corporal Lewis and the entire Royal Grenada Police Force. The police officer looked at the angry man and was glad that he had called for backup. The conductor would have to spend some time in the cell and pay a fine for using offensive language and assaulting an officer.

"Conductor, we have to take you in," Lewis said. He turned to Joseph. "Driver, please control your guy."

"Officer, you really unfair," Joseph replied. "All of us trying to eat ah food. You know how the economy is already."

"That does not give you the right to break the law," the corporal retorted. "You put a lot of people lives in danger. The road is not yours alone!"

The police officer paused for a moment before continuing.

"I have to report you for dangerous driving. In fact, I arresting you for that. And I also reporting you for not completing your bus route. That sticker on your windshield says you have to reach Calliste to complete the route."

Joseph growled. "So just for that little move you arrestin' me?"

"Driver, you didn't notice how hard a couple cars had to jam brakes when you come down on the north-bound side?"

"But no accident take place! I don't know why all-you police can't leave us bus-men alone."

Corporal Lewis chuckled as he wrote in his little black book.

"Mr. Joseph, you will get a summons within fourteen days to appear in court to answer charges of dangerous driving and for failing to complete your route."

The conductor paced the sidewalk alongside the bus, breathing heavily, clenching his fists and contracting his biceps and pecs. Corporal Lewis eyed him suspiciously. He placed his right hand on the butt of his sidearm. He thanked the Commissioner for successfully making a case to government for all motor officers to wear body cams when patrolling the nation's roads.

"Conductor, please sit in the bus!" the officer ordered.

The conductor froze in mid-step and regarded the policeman with a frown. The bus driver's eyes swept back and forth between his conductor and Corporal Lewis.

"Justin, just do what the officer say, eh" the driver said. "I ain' want trouble here today."

Justin threw his head back and screamed then sat silently in the bus. A marked police car with flashing lights approached them, driving against the north-flowing traffic.

"Corporal, you need some help with dem fellas?" A constable jumped out of the sedan while a burly sergeant squeezed out of the driver's seat.

"I arresting the conductor here for using obscene and threatening language towards an officer," Corporal Lewis replied. "And the driver is also under arrest for dangerous driving."

"Officer Thomas, deal with the traffic please," the sergeant ordered the constable before consulting with Lewis.

"Corporal, what the driver do that so dangerous that you have to arrest him?"

Lewis reported what he had witnessed about twenty minutes ago when the bus crossed illegally from the airport-bound to the city-bound lanes, and the effect that manoeuvre had on the flow of traffic. The sergeant agreed that the motor officer had sufficient grounds to arrest the bus driver.

The flashing lights of the police car attracted quite a bit of attention. Cars slowed and pedestrians snapped pictures with their mobile devices. Buses honked their horns loudly as they crawled past the scene. Some conductors cursed at the police officers while others jeered at Justin and Joseph. Corporal Lewis knew that social media would be alive tonight with pictures and videos of this scene.

"Conductor, stand up and put your hands behind your back!" the sergeant commanded.

Corporal Lewis informed the bus operators about the reasons for their arrest.

"Mr. Joseph, I will drive back with you in your bus to the station," the sergeant said. "We following the police car. And make sure you turn on the a/c."

A few minutes later, Justin sat in the back seat of the air-conditioned police car in a two-vehicle convoy heading towards the South St. George Police Station in Morne Rouge. Corporal Lewis resumed patrolling Zone One. This vital artery connected the nation's capital to its international airport. He circled back to the south-bound lanes of The Stretch to head to the Maurice Bishop International Airport in Point Salines. He intended to use the time to better familiarise himself with his powerful machine.

Lewis was one of six motor officers who had been specially trained to operate the BMW R1200RT-P. On ceremonial occasions, the six outriders would escort the Governor General and/or the Prime Minister to special events like the opening of Parliament, or the Independence Parade. The six officers had undergone nine months of intense training in England, and later, at the obstacle course set up at the old Pearls airstrip in St. Andrew's.

Corporal Lewis couldn't help grinning again as he recalled the intense friendly rivalry to determine unofficially who was the best police outrider. He looked at his dash as he followed a silver Hyundai Tucson. The Tucson cruised down the highway with its windows rolled up. Lewis frowned as he thought about how much gas that driver was burning with the a/c on. He checked the digital display for the recorded speed of the silver vehicle. He whistled at what he thought was an accurate reading. The Tucson turned left towards St. George's University at the True Blue round-about.

Continuing right, toward the Maurice Bishop International Airport on the southernmost tip of the island, Corporal Lewis accelerated to eighty kilometres per hour then hit the cruise-control switch on his left handlebar. He toggled another switch on the same handlebar to lift the windscreen. With the bike now in Dynamic mode, he activated its emergency lights but kept the siren off. Even in the bright sunlight, the Code Three brilliant red and blue flashing LED's mounted above the left and right front turn signals, respectively, would alert any driver of the approaching emergency vehicle.

"Woii!" the officer exclaimed. "Valentino Rossi, *wi*!" He chuckled inside his helmet as the BMW ate up the highway. He covered the 2.5 km to the airport in less than two minutes.

At the airport, Lewis used the washroom then visited with an old schoolmate at the security office. He also took the opportunity to hydrate himself. Twenty minutes later, he returned to patrolling the busy Grand Anse road, heading north towards Grenada's capital. A convoy of four buses crept in the heavy south-bound traffic as he rode past Excel Plaza. He hoped 2017 would bring the inconsiderate bus drivers to their senses. Less than a minute later, a black bus pulled out of a bus-stop and merged into traffic without signalling. An inconvenienced driver veered away from the fully-loaded vehicle and leaned on his horn. The bus-driver flung his arm dismissively in the direction of the angry honking. The corporal exhaled audibly but refrained from chasing the bus. *If I report him for driving without due care and attention, he go say I unfair.*

The motor officer pulled into the bus-stop at the major intersection of the entrances to the

Radisson Hotel on one side, and the Grand Anse Shopping Centre on the other. He planned to spend a few minutes regulating the buses that used this stop. Many had a habit of practically parking in the middle of the busy junction or blocking the entrance to the hotel.

Corporal Lewis eyed six pedestrians on the other side of the road waiting for all lights to change to red before they crossed. He pulled off his gloves then strolled to the entrance of the bus-stop. Four wide-bodied Toyota Hiace buses approached, the first one coming to a standstill as close to the intersection as possible. Lewis motioned to the driver to move to the other end of the bus-stop. A loud steupse floated out of that bus, but the driver complied. Lewis directed the other three buses to pull in behind the first bus in single file formation. No one was happier than the operators of the fourth bus whose conductor hopped out grinning at his three competitors ahead of him. All four doormen shuffled to the intersection as quickly as possible. The police officer gritted his teeth as each young man held up his pants whose belt rested below the buttocks, brightly-coloured boxers on full display. *I wish I coulda charge dem fellas for indecency*, he thought. A blue Hiace raced up and stopped behind the last passenger vehicle, albeit in the intersection, its electronic horn deafening the corporal.

"Driver, you name on the dotish list or wha'?" Corporal Lewis said to the slim man behind the wheel.

A young lady sitting directly behind the driver burst out laughing, tears streaking her makeup as they flowed down her face.

The driver scowled at the motor officer and pointed to the buses ahead of him. "You kyaann' see the bus-stop full up?"

Lewis laughed. "Driver, it have four bus on the stop; all ah dem have plenty room. You watching six people over dey. You kyaann' do Maths?"

The young lady now collapsed onto the floor of the bus, holding her sides and coughing between cackles.

The driver rolled his eyes. He called out to his conductor who had earlier leapt out to try to coax the waiting pedestrians to his bus. The chubby youth jogged back to his vehicle, pulling up his drooping but skinny pants as he climbed aboard. Corporal Lewis stared at him as his bus pulled out into traffic and headed in the direction of St. George's.

"Wow! Babe, a BMWR twelve hundred RT!"

The British accent reached the corporal's ears causing him to whirl around. A momentary wave of confusion flooded his face as he saw a black couple admiring the pride of the Royal Grenada Police Force. He smiled as he approached them. The man, who appeared to be in his sixties, studied the RGPF motorman.

"Officer, you got a sweet machine there."

"Thank you, Sir. You're a biker?"

"Twenty years with the Special Escort Group of the London Metropolitan Police Service! But this is much better than what we used in the seventies and eighties." He nodded towards Lewis' bike.

Corporal Lewis eyeballed the visitor with great admiration and respect. "The SEG? Woiii! Did you ever escort the Queen?"

The Briton laughed. "Oh, no. But I was on a team that escorted Thatcher in eighty-one."

Lewis conversed with the Englishman for a few minutes while keeping an eye on the intersection.

A loud boom shook the area and the Briton ducked behind the corporal's bike pulling his wife down with him. Lewis stooped, his hand reaching for his sidearm. The mirror of one of the buses shattered. Two teenage girls standing under the shed at the bus-stop screamed. All eyes turned in the direction of the source of the sound.

A white Toyota Corolla peeled around two vehicles that had pulled up at the north-bound red light, the heavy bassline of a rap tune pouring out of its open windows. The impatient driver sped through the lights barely missing a Hyundai Accent about to take the right turn from the Shopping Centre. The Accent screeched to a halt in the middle of the intersection. Its engine sputtered then died. The elderly female driver trembled uncontrollably.

Corporal Lewis dashed over to her. "Ma'am, you okay?"

"Yes, me son. I thought that car would hit me."

The police officer smiled. "Those young fellas really reckless. Take your time and drive over to the bus-stop here."

The lady restarted the car and Lewis guided her to park within the bus-stop zone, and off the roadway. He glared in the direction of the disappearing Corolla then sprinted to his bike.

The BMW shot up the straight section of road like an arrow, dodging potholes and zooming past stationary vehicles that snaked along the south-bound lane. Lewis vowed to catch that inconsiderate driver. He hoped the car hadn't disappeared into one of the many sideroads between Grand Anse and St. George's. He hit his siren and darted around a slow-moving taxi. Just as he was about to lose hope, he heard a faint bassline. The song, that only minutes ago had disrupted the smooth flow of traffic at the Radisson lights, became progressively louder. Within a minute, he had the white car in his sights and activated his body cam. The driver appeared to be ignoring the piercing wails of the siren, and the bright flashing lights, so Lewis pulled alongside the front window and jabbed his finger towards the curb. The car ground to a halt after forty metres.

Twenty minutes later, the teenage driver was staring out of the back window of a police van on his way to the Central Police Station on The Carenage. Tears flowed copiously from his eyes. A police wrecker towed the mobile boombox to an impound facility.

"I hope he could pay that one thousand dollars for driving without a licence," Corporal Lewis said as he watched the teen's gloomy face. He sighed as he thought about the other heavy fine the youth had to deal with for the excessive noise that came from the vehicle. "I know he can't take the alternative six months in prison."

****

"Officer, Officer, help me cross, nuh!" a lady called out as Lewis cruised along the Kirani James Boulevard. He came to a halt in front of the middle-aged pedestrian.

"Yes, Ma'am," the corporal said. "You trying to cross the road?"

"Look how long I stand up here and nobody stopping to let me cross."

Lewis looked around then hung his head. The white stripes of a pedestrian crossing less than five metres from them threatened to blind him in the bright sunlight.

"Ma'am, all you have to do is use the crossing right there." The policeman pointed to the crosswalk.

The lady scowled at him. "So, you want me to walk back all over dey to cross the road?"

The officer forced a smile. "Ma'am, that is the designated area for people to cross. Please use it."

Grumbling, the lady took eight steps to reach the crosswalk. Cars from each direction promptly stopped for her to access the other side of the road.

"Boy, some people real slack." Corporal Lewis shook his head as he resumed his patrol, heading back to Grand Anse. His fingers drummed a rhythm on his handlebars as he hummed a Christmas *parang* soca.

Lewis' mind floated to the five NBA games he intended to watch on Christmas day. He tried to predict which teams would win. *I know the Warriors winning for sure*, he thought. He also ruminated about the Grenadian novel he intended to read tonight. A few officers had convinced him to read *White Spice*, a crime thriller they guaranteed he wouldn't be able to put down. A couple of his colleagues had confessed to reading the book three times. He grinned as his mind switched to Christmas-day meals. Kenisha had invited him over for lunch at one p.m. He also had an invitation to dinner at Antonia's at eight. *Plenty eating tomorrow*, he chuckled as he imagined baked chicken, curried goat, potato salad, macaroni pie, coleslaw, baked ham, stew goat, and ground provision.

He intended to enjoy plenty sorrel, wine and black cake as well.

"No way!" Corporal Lewis touched the power button of his body camera.

A white package flew out of a car that approached the motor officer from the opposite direction. Lewis estimated that he was about thirty-five metres away, so he switched on his lights and siren, and played "chicken" with the oncoming vehicle to stop the litterbugs.

Three teenage girls stared up at him as he inspected the driver's documents.

"You-all know why I stop you?"

"Because Lynn not wearing seatbelt?" the girl at the back replied, laughing.

Corporal Lewis rolled his eyes. "Well, that is an offence too. So, Lynn could be fined one thousand dollars. But who pelt that package out of the car?"

Silence reigned for a full minute.

"Look, Ladies," Lewis began. "Littering is not just a crime. It's bad for the environment. You have two choices: receive a heavy fine for littering, or go and pick up the trash you throw out back there." He nodded in the direction of the discarded item.

Doors flew open and the young ladies hurried back to where they had ejected the trash. After two minutes, they returned to Corporal Lewis and their car, their arms overflowing with fast-food packages. The officer frowned then smirked.

"Good job, Ladies!"

The teens stared at the ground.

"What school you-all go to?

"The T.A. Marryshow Community College," the driver said softly.

"Nice! And what's your major?"

"Environmental Science."

Corporal Lewis stared at the girl and sighed. "Girls, I won't charge you today since you did some community service just now. But never litter again. Is that clear?"

"Yes, Sir!" a chorus of voices sang.

The corporal watched as the girls snapped seatbelts into place and prepared to take off towards St. George's. The sounds of racing engines reached his ears seconds before a white blur and a silver streak zipped by.

"Wait!" he shouted, putting out a hand to prevent the girls from moving off.

The environmentalist screamed as a rush of air shook her coupe.

"Well why dem buses driving so crazy?" Lewis said. "They want to kill somebody on this Christmas Eve?"

He grabbed his radio to alert any patrols between Belmont and St. George's to stop and detain the drivers of the two buses for speeding and reckless driving. His blood froze as the silver Toyota Hiace veered around its rival who travelled at about seventy kilometres per hour. Lewis growled. *Like dem boy forget this is a two-lane road!* The van's trombone-sounding horn blared, as if the driver thought that would clear the lane of oncoming traffic as he approached a shallow corner. A weaker tooting challenged the deafening sound as a black Hummer H3T, cruising south, filled the entire lane. Lewis realised that wide-bodied vehicles could never fit three-abreast on this two-lane road. Tyres from both vehicles screeched on the black tar, causing the motor officer to think of a bass vocalist and a soprano performing a duet. The bus slammed head-on into the Hummer at forty kilometres per hour, pushing the heavy mid-sized pickup truck backwards a few metres. The front of the bus crumpled like cardboard as it wrapped around the chrome bumper and grill of the H3T. Both front tyres of the Toyota popped.

"Noooooooooooo!" Corporal Lewis yelled as he rushed to his bike. He thanked God that he hadn't switched off his bodycam after dealing with the girls.

The high-speed collision between the Hummer and the speeding bus created an explosion that brought people running out of nearby houses. The flow of traffic in all directions halted immediately. A blood-curdling bellow leapt out of the bus, joined by high-pitched screams, and loud groans.

Corporal Lewis thought it took him half a day to cover the sixty metres to the accident site. He radioed for paramedics, fire/rescue, and an investigative unit from the Traffic Department. He advised the dispatcher to send all the available ambulances from the General Hospital. He also suggested that extra officers be sent to redirect traffic to other routes. He sighed as he realised he would have to deal with the scene alone until backup arrived in about fifteen minutes.

Corporal Lewis almost threw up when he peered into the front of the bus. The steering wheel now rested a few centimetres inside the driver's chest while his shoulders seemed to have disappeared inside his seat. Blood flowed out of his mouth and nostrils. The young man's eyes fluttered continuously and his bellows had now become whimpers. He coughed occasionally.

"Help coming soon," Lewis said. "What's your name?"

"Leroy," the driver said after a short coughing fit.

"Okay, Leroy. Try to stay awake. I think I hear the ambulance."

Lewis looked down at Leroy's legs and gulped as he saw that the driver and the bus had become one. He pleaded silently for an ambulance to get to the scene right now. Another motor bike pulled up and Lewis nodded at the rider as he recognised an on-duty plain-clothes officer from his station.

"Martin, boy, I glad to see you. Bring your first-aid kit and check those three people in the back of this bus. We can't move the driver, but he hurt real bad."

Lewis dashed over to the Hummer. The middle-aged driver groaned and rocked his head from side to side. The police officer squirmed inwardly at the sight of a bloody nose and swollen eyelid. He noted the deflated and red-stained airbag.

"Mister, don't move. Ambulance on the way."

"I can't move. I think me foot break."

"Corporal, we have three people with head injuries here," Martin called out.

"Okay. Come over here and help me with this driver."

The two policemen pulled the man gingerly from his vehicle and laid him flat on the ground.

"Try to stay awake, Sir," Lewis advised. "Can you tell me your name?"

"Wildman."

"Mr. Wildman, help is on the way."

The sound of sirens filled the air as emergency vehicles picked their way cautiously through parked vehicles and a crowd of curious onlookers. Two units from the Traffic Department followed the ambulances.

A male voice cried out for his mother. A team of paramedics headed for the passenger compartment of the bus as soon as their ambulance came to a stop.

"Only two ambulance they send?" Martin growled.

Inspector Mitchell assumed command of the scene. He directed Lewis and Martin to redirect traffic on each side of the impact site to turn around and use alternative routes to their destinations.

"And set up a perimeter of sixty metres," the Inspector instructed.

The two motor officers jogged off in opposite directions with spools of yellow caution tape.

The team of firefighters worked diligently to cut the bus open. After enduring advice, suggestions and insults from onlookers for over twenty minutes, the team that included paramedics finally pulled the unconscious bus-driver out of his seat and began resuscitation procedures.

"He lose real blood," an accompanying nurse announced.

Soon, one ambulance sped off with the critically-wounded patient.

"I really hope he will live to see 2017," Corporal Lewis said. "Why fellas can't take their time on the road?"

"You mean you hope he see Christmas," Martin said.

The paramedics from the other ambulance confirmed that Mr. Wildman had suffered a dislocated ankle. They also concluded that he had experienced a concussion when the airbag went off. The ambulance headed for the General Hospital in the city with Mr. Wildman and two injured passengers from the bus. A police car followed the ambulance, carrying the third injured fare.

"Mr. Lewis, tell me what happen here, nuh," Inspector Mitchell called out.

Corporal Lewis spent a couple minutes relating what he had witnessed. "And I have it all on my bodycam."

"So where is the other bus that Leroy was racing with?" Mitchell inquired.

"That one must be reach in town already," Lewis said. "He partly to blame for this accident and he didn't even stop or turn back."

"Well, some people will get some serious charges today," Mitchell said. "Including that injured driver. If he survive."

Lewis and Mitchell looked at each other and exhaled simultaneously.

"When you return to the station later, download the footage quick and let me see it," Mitchell said. "We go arrest that other bus driver after we identify he bus."

Inspector Mitchell released Corporal Lewis and Constable Martin to resume patrolling Zone One.

"This could take a couple hours to sort out," the inspector said, waving his hand over the accident site.

The corporal continued his patrol, heading towards Grand Anse. He admired the sailboats anchored just offshore in the Caribbean Sea while trying to forget about the horrific scene he had just witnessed. He vowed to take a dip on the beach on Christmas morning. He frowned as two people stopped a bus that travelled two vehicles ahead of him. Lewis activated his siren, and his bodycam.

"Driver, you mean a fine of $1500 is worth picking up a fare of five dollars?" the officer asked as he wrote in his book five minutes later. "I charging both you and the conductor for picking up passengers in a non-designated area."

The big-belly man pouted as he stared straight ahead.

"Conductor, please drop the people you just picked up," Corporal Lewis ordered.

The teenage conductor opened the side door but remained in his seat. The couple who had most recently boarded the bus refused to step out. The conductor looked to his driver for help but the latter ignored him.

"Well, Officer, dem people doh want to come out," the conductor said.

"You know, the law should start charging people too, for boarding buses off the bus stop," the corporal said.

Lewis finished writing then turned his attention to the passengers. He stared at the man who had entered a few minutes ago. Complete silence enveloped the bus for the duration of the stare-down. He put his hand on his sidearm. A male passenger screamed. The young conductor retreated further inside his bus, fear written all over his face. The two people changed their minds and rushed out of the vehicle.

"Watch, I doh want to get shoot here today!" the lady declared.

"Driver, please continue," Lewis said after he determined that the couple stood safely away from the bus. The copper-coloured vehicle moved off.

"What a day!" Lewis muttered while looking at his watch. "Only two more hours before I done patrolling, *wi*."

"Looks like somebody having car trouble," Corporal Lewis mouthed silently as he observed an SUV sitting in the southbound bus-stop at the Radisson traffic lights. He pulled up behind the yellow Kia Sportage and touched the power button on his bodycam.

Lewis tapped on the tinted front passenger window. It slid down and his eyes drifted past the empty passenger seat to fall on a pair of smooth chocolate thighs that disappeared into the blue skirt of a business suit. He greeted the driver who texted rapidly on a phone.

"Miss, you okay?"

"What is it?"

Lewis raised an eyebrow. "You having car trouble?"

"No, Officer, I just stop to send an important message."

Corporal Lewis frowned. "Miss, this is a bus-stop. You can't take up space here just to use your phone. Please move along!"

The lady glared at the policeman. "Officer, how you expect me to text and drive? I pull into a safe spot off the road but you harassing me. What wrong with all-you?"

"Miss, I could charge you for parking on a bus-stop. If you did your driver's exam you would know you cannot stop at a bus-stop. People always saying bus-men like to block traffic. Now you taking up their space. Lemme tell you one more time, please move along!"

The lady swore under her breath before rolling up the electric-powered window, leaving the police officer to stare at his own face. She pulled into the roadway without checking the traffic. Corporal Lewis thanked God that for that ten seconds on this Christmas Eve, the flow of traffic at this intersection paused. He mopped his brow and decided to get some coconut water at the next bus-stop.

Lewis sucked up the refreshing liquid directly from a coconut gourd while observing the traffic at the Morne Rouge round-about. Nearby, Wall Street bustled with pedestrians. The officer imagined how the scene looked from above. A truck's horn drowned out any other sound in the area. The corporal turned to see a thirty-two-ton Mack lorry approaching the north-bound bus stop, its path impeded by a bus that had stopped in the roadway and within the round-about zone. The truck-driver blasted his horn a couple more times. The bus-conductor ignored the massive vehicle as he called potential passengers on Wall Street. Air brakes hissed. The truck-driver cursed.

Corporal Lewis observed the showdown as he savoured his coconut water. *Now this should be interesting,* he thought with a sneer.

The loaded truck lurched forward a few times but the bus refused to move. Screeching tyres, hissing air, honking horns, shouts and screams flooded the space. Lewis almost dropped his coconut. He grinned.

"Officer, you stand up dey laughing?" a man said. "You want the truck to mash up the bus?"

"That truck doing what most drivers always want to do."

The Mack had inched up to the bus and gently pushed it forward a few metres. Shocked passengers screamed at the bus driver to make way for the behemoth. The truck's ear-splitting horn scared them even more. The bus-driver finally pulled out of the roadway and the massive truck moved along. Lewis could swear that he heard the truck-driver laughing. The bus-driver ran across the road to him.

"Officer, you ain' see wha' dat truck do me bus?"

"Driver, you were blocking the road and trying to pick up people. If you had pulled out of the road and into the designated bus-stop, that would not happen. I should actually be charging you. That's a fine of $1500."

The bus driver slinked back to his vehicle.

"That good for you," a lady said. "All-you always blocking the road and holding up traffic."

"People, I have work to do," Corporal Lewis said. He thanked the coconut vendor and sped off.

The motor officer decided to patrol Lance aux Epines for the final half-hour of his shift. He radioed his base to apprise the dispatcher of his plans then entered the Beverly Hills of Grenada. He marvelled at the huge mansions that dotted the roadside and hillside. He zipped past the lone church in the area, and chuckled as the fortified American embassy came into view, a "Stars and Stripes" fluttering majestically above the green building. *Overkill.* A jogger approaching from the opposite direction, stopped, and flagged him down. He had to gear down progressively to finally pull up directly in front of the man.

"Is everything okay?" the man asked, his hands on his waist.

"Er, yes, Sir." Lewis scrutinised him. "Why?"

"It's just that I have never ever seen a police patrol down here during the day."

Corporal Lewis laughed. "Nah, man. We come down here from time to time."

The man snickered. "Okay, Officer. Have a good day!"

An annoyed Corporal Lewis continued his ride into Lance aux Epines for half a minute more then turned around and sped back towards Grand Anse. As he zipped by the jogger, he touched his siren. The man jumped, and dove into the nearby bush. Lewis laughed loudly.

"Time to head back to Central," he muttered. "I getting hungry now." He did not intend to stop between Grand Anse and the Carenage.

"Holy cow! Now this I have to record." The policeman's hand drifted to his camera.

A red "old-school" Toyota drove slowly ahead of the BMW motorbike, its back bumper almost touching the road surface. Corporal

Lewis moved closer and was shocked to see six people sitting in the back row meant to hold three passengers comfortably. The vehicle was overloaded! The conductor's entire upper body hung outside the bus, facing backwards. Lewis blasted his siren three times and the bus pulled to the side of the road and stopped. His eyes bugged when he saw two plump ladies sitting up front with the driver.

"Everybody, please get out," the policeman commanded. "Driver, that's an accident waiting to happen."

The vehicle rose visibly as the twenty-nine passengers alighted. Corporal Lewis could have sworn that he'd heard the bus groan. He couldn't hide his amusement as some passengers stretched and cracked a few joints.

"Looks like I did some of you a favour," he said to the crowd. "Driver, lemme see the particulars."

"Frederick Charles," he read from the driver's license. "You know I have to charge you for overload. You're insured to carry seventeen passengers."

"But officer, I was driving slow," Charles protested. "Nobody was in danger."

"Everybody was in danger, Mr. Charles," Corporal Lewis growled as he wrote in his black book. "And those two ladies up front weren't even wearing seat belts. I have to charge them too."

"I tell the conductor we full but he keep saying we could take one more."

"Conductor, I charging you too," Lewis said to skinny youth. "All-you know Grand Anse have a lot of buses. You coulda leave some people for dem other buses."

The conductor opened his mouth in a silent bawl, holding his head with both hands.

"People, all-you better catch other buses," the policeman advised.

The conductor stepped forward with his money-bag and an open palm, and approached the passengers.

"Seriously?" Corporal Lewis said. "You drop dem people in town?"

The conductor frowned but did not protest.

Fifteen minutes later, Corporal Lewis pulled into the Traffic Department at Central Police Station.

"Inspector, all kinda craziness take place in Zone One today, *wi*," Lewis greeted his supervisor.

The inspector grinned. "Ah go read it in you report. And make haste download the footage from you bodycam."

THE END

ZONE ONE

Zone One – Grand Anse, St. George's

ZONE ONE

ABOUT THE AUTHOR

D. E. Ambrose is an educator and author from the Caribbean island of Grenada. He is a Communication Studies lecturer at the T.A. Marryshow Community College. He also teaches Spanish, French and German at the college.

Ambrose is the author of *White Spice* (2015) and *That Time in Bogles – A Carriacou Tale* (2018).

Made in the USA
Columbia, SC
17 November 2023